This book belongs to

_____

The Adventures of

Bella & Harry

Let's Visit Istanbul!

Written By

Lisa Manzione

Illustrated By

Kristine Lucco

Bella & Harry, LLC

www.BellaAndHarry.com
email: BellaAndHarryGo@aol.com

Merhaba, friends!
Harry and I are glad you decided to join us on our family adventure today!

Right now, we are going for a ferry ride on the Bosphorus River (or Bosphorus Strait) in Istanbul, Turkey!

5

"Bella, I love ferry rides, don't you?"

"Yes I do, especially early in the morning! Harry, look over there! What a cool bridge! There are two bridges that currently cross the Bosphorus. The name of this bridge is the First Bosphorus Bridge.

This bridge connects the continent of Asia to the continent of Europe."

6

"**Ortakoy**, a neighborhood in Istanbul, is our first stop!"

"**Everybody** off the boat!"

"Bella, what is that cool building I see near the shore of the Bosphorus?"

"Harry, that building is called the Grand Imperial Mosque of Sultan Abdülmecid and is sometimes called the Ortakoy Mosque."

"**A** mosque, Bella? What is a mosque?"

"Well Harry, a mosque is a building used for those who practice
the Muslim faith. There are many different faiths in our world today
and each faith or religion has its own buildings for worship.
There are over 3,000 mosques in Istanbul."

"**Let's** go Harry! We are stopping for breakfast at a restaurant near the Bosphorus. Our children are going to have a traditional Turkish breakfast."

"**What** are they having for breakfast Bella?"

"They are having menemen, which is eggs, onions, peppers and tomatoes, with other spices, all mixed together and scrambled. They are also having simit, a type of bread that is topped with sesame seeds and formed into a ring before baking. Plus, cheese, yogurt and honey... all of your favorites Harry!"

11

"**Come** on Harry! We are off to see the Topkapi Palace! A place where Sultans lived in the past! Sultans do not live here anymore. It is a museum now."

"**Bella**, I know what a Sultan is! A Sultan is a ruler!"

"Yes, Harry! A Sultan is a King or ruler, usually of a Muslim country."

"**Look** Harry, another palace! It's Dolmabahce Palace! This palace, which is now a museum, is located on the bank of the Bosphorus. How beautiful!"

"Let's play chase! You are it Bella!"

"**Let's** go Harry! Our tour is moving on. We are heading to one of the oldest and biggest covered markets in the world... The Grand Bazaar."

"**Now** Harry, you know the rules. We must stay together. The Grand Bazaar has over 60 streets and over 5,000 vendors selling carpets, hand painted ceramics, and all sorts of other things. There are four main gates to enter and exit the Grand Bazaar, so we could easily get lost."

TURKISH HANDBAGS

17

"WOW, Bella! This place is so cool! I feel like I am going back in time. Bella, do you think we will see a flying magic carpet? I really want to fly on a magic carpet!"

18

"Ha! Ha! Harry, carpets do not fly!"

"Oh, really?"

19

Later in the day, Bella found herself
staring at the pretty lights with many colors of cut glass.

She did not notice her family was leaving.
Suddenly, Bella was all alone!

Bella looked to the left!

Bella looked to the right!
No family! Where could they have gone?

"Harry!"

21

Bella started to run as fast as she could through the bazaar.
She was frightened!

Suddenly, Bella saw Harry and her family looking at the beautiful carpets.

22

"**Whew!** I am glad I found you!!
Harry, what are you doing on that carpet?"

"Bella, I really want to ride a magic carpet!"

"Oh Harry! I told you, carpets don't fly!!!"

"Bella, you also told me that 'we must stay
together' and that 'we could easily get lost.'"

23

"Come on Harry! We are going to the Egyptian or Spice Market now."

"Egyptian Market, Bella? I thought we were in Istanbul, Turkey?"

"Harry, we are in Turkey. The market was first called the Egyptian Market because a lot of the spices came from Egypt, India and Southeast Asia hundreds of years ago."

24

"**Istanbul** is a very old city and has played a big role in history. Did you know, hundreds of years ago, Istanbul was called Constantinople?"

"Hmm... no, I did not know that Bella."

"Harry, we are stopping to have tea and Turkish Delight or Lokum, a Turkish gel-like candy that is sometimes covered in powdered sugar."

"Bella, this tastes great! Do you think we can find a magic carpet to ride after our snack?"

"No Harry, I have told you, there are no magic carpets!!!"

BLACK SEA

EUROPE

ISTANBUL

ASIA

TURKEY

MEDITERRANEAN
SEA

SYRIA

IRAQ

"**Harry**, let's sit down
and look at this map. As I said
before, Turkey is on both the
Asian continent and the European
continent. Here is Istanbul."

"**Snack** time is over. We are off to see another famous landmark, the Blue Mosque."

"**Harry**, the Blue Mosque got its name because of the blue tiles on the inside of the walls. The Blue Mosque is different than most mosques because it has six minarets. Minarets are tall, slender towers with balconies from which people are called to prayer several times daily."

"**Next** Harry, we are off to see the Hagia Sophia. First it was a church, then a mosque and now a museum. The Hagia Sophia is located within the first of the seven hills of Istanbul."

"**The** old city of Constantinople was built on seven hills, circled by a city wall, just like old Rome. There is a lot of history in Turkey, but it looks like we are heading back to our hotel now. Whew! What a busy day!"

We had a great time with you in Istanbul but for now, it is 'Elveda' or good-bye in Turkish from Bella Boo and Harry too! See you on our next adventure!

Our Adventures in Turkey

Bella loves wearing traditional "Evil Eye" jewelry!

Harry performs with the "Whirling Dervishes" while in Cappadocia, Turkey.

Bella and Harry visit the "Library of Celsus" in Ephesus, Turkey.

Bella and Harry loved their visit to Cappadocia, Turkey. Cappadocia is also known as the "Land of Fairy Chimneys". What a great place for a balloon ride!

34

Fun Turkish Words and Phrases

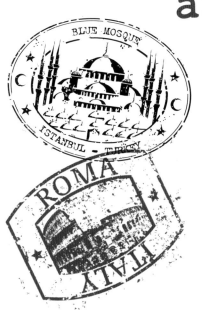

Girl dog – Kiz köpek

Boy dog – Erkek köpek

Please – Lütfen

Yes – Evet

No – Hayir

Hello – Merhaba

Good-bye – Elveda

Requests for permission to make copies of any part of the work should be directed to BellaAndHarryGo@aol.com or 855-235-5211.

Library of Congress Cataloging-in-Publications Data is available

Manzione, Lisa

The Adventures of Bella & Harry: Let's Visit Istanbul!

ISBN: 978-1-937616-09-0

First Edition

Book Nine of Bella & Harry Series

For further information please visit:

www.BellaAndHarry.com

or

Email: BellaAndHarryGo@aol.com

CPSIA Section 103 (a) Compliant

www.beaconstar.com/ consumer

ID: L0118329. Tracking No.: MR28582-1-9183

Printed in China

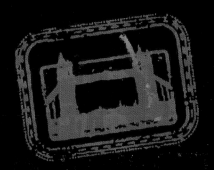